GROSSET & DUNLAP
Penguin Young Readers Group
An Imprint of Penguin Random House LLC

Copyright © 2015 by Eric Carle LLC. ERIC CARLE's name and signature logotype are trademarks of Eric Carle. All rights reserved. Published by Grosset & Dunlap, an imprint of Penguin Random House LLC, 345 Hudson Street, New York, New York 10014. GROSSET & DUNLAP is a trademark of Penguin Random House LLC. Manufactured in China.

Library of Congress Cataloging-in-Publication Data is available.

ISBN 978-0-448-48932-2   10 9 8 7 6 5 4 3

from The Very Hungry Caterpillar

Eric Carle

Grosset & Dunlap
An Imprint of Penguin Random House

You are . . .

...so
sweet

...the cherry
on my cake

. . . the apple
of my eye

. . . the

bee's

knees.

You make . . .

. . . the sun
shine brighter

... the stars
sparkle

. . . the **birds** sing

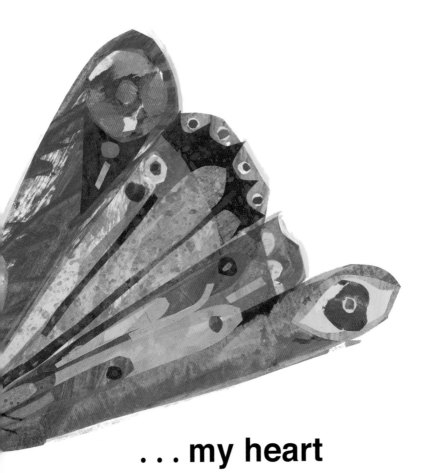

. . . my heart

flutter.

That's **why**...